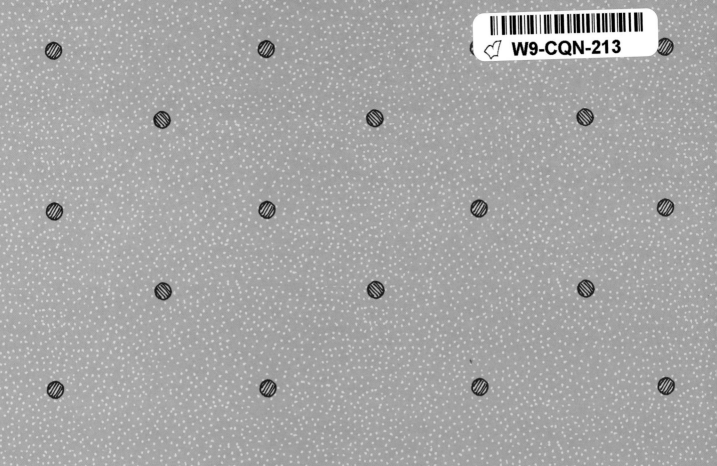

We thank the Cultural Institute of King's College, London for supporting this project.

Where has the Tiger gone?

Copyright © 2018 Tara Books Pvt. Ltd.

Text and Illustrations: Dhavat Singh Uikey
Design: Ragini Siruguri

For this edition:
Tara Books Pvt. Ltd., India <www.tarabooks.com>
and
Tara Publishing Ltd., UK <www.tarabooks.com/uk>

Production: C. Arumugam
Printed in India by Canara Traders and Printers

ISBN 978-93-83145-99-7

Where has the Tiger gone?

Dhavat Singh Uikey

Tiger Memories

THE TIGER IS IMPORTANT to all Gond people. There are several groups and clans among the Gonds, and my community, for example, is called Pardhan. We used to be bards and singers, and for us, the tiger was always part of the natural world. In the way that we worship the earth, a river, a tree or the sun, we also respect and value the tiger. For the Khushram clan amongst us, the tiger is a god known as Bagaisur. For the Shyams, the tiger is the vehicle on which their tutelary goddess Durga rides.

We value, but we also fear the tiger. When I was a child, I would go with my parents and other village elders to pick firewood. We would first climb one hill—called Donger—then make our way to another, which was known as Dadar. Before entering the forest, the elders would always place a log of wood as an offering under a tree. When I asked what this meant, I was told that since we were going to go into the jungle—which was a dangerous place—we were praying to the forest goddess to keep an eye on us. I also remember that in some other places, we offered a stone to the goddess. But despite the fact that we prayed and asked for protection, the tiger was still a creature that we worried about. Maybe that's why the tiger figured so prominently in the songs and stories of the Pardhans.

There is a story about how the Pardhans became story-tellers and musicians.

Once upon a time there lived a Gond with his wife, the Gondin. They had six sons. They lived in a village and farmed for a living. During one harvest season, when their crop of rice was almost ready, they decided to move out of their house, to live in the rice field. They wanted to guard their ripening crop from marauding animals, so they built a platform from where they could keep watch. At that time the Gondin was pregnant, and about to give birth, but she insisted on helping the family with the harvest.

It was soon time to reap, and they began to harvest the crop. Just as they were half way through, the Gondin gave birth to a boy. But the work had to continue, so the child was put to sleep in a straw winnow, and placed on top of a tall heap of grain.

The Gondin's other children, the six sons, told their father that the youngest ought to be named 'Par (outside) Dhan (grain)' since he was born outdoors, amidst the grain.

'He cannot live with us, nor can he eat with us, for he belongs to the outside. Since he was born when half the grain was harvested and half was left, we'll give him half a share of everything.'

And so the child called Pardhan remained outside, and soon learned to play a stringed instrument, called the bana. He became adept at it, but for other things he continued to be dependent on his brothers. It is said that ever since then, there have always been Pardhans amongst the Gonds. The Pardhans would play, sing and entertain the community—but they would also put their hands to the plough when it was needed, just like the others.

The Pardhans were clever. They would embellish their tales with jokes, rumours and even add a fake incident or two. They paid periodic visits to important Gond households in different places, where they would tell stories the whole night, to the entire village. Their talk was so entertaining that their listeners would be completely entranced. For those returning home at the end of a long day's work, after walking through forests and fields, the Pardhan's songs and stories would lighten the hours. The Pardhans performed other functions in the community as well. For instance, they would be the accompanying musicians at village festivals and dances. Or when someone had passed away, they would keep watch with the family of the deceased, singing and lightening the grief-stricken mood. They would often sit around all night, drinking Mahua, and the words and music would go on until the cock crowed and the day dawned. They have always had a strong sense of community.

Some things have changed over time, and most Pardhans now work in the fields to make a living. Yet they still remain the storytellers and cultural keepers of the community, but in a different way. For instance, they have taken to telling stories through painting, and many Pardhans have become well-known artists. Pardhan homes are beautifully decorated with murals and paintings—of birds, animals, or gods and the courtyards are decorated with the traditional floor art called Digna.

I am a Pardhan, from the village of Patangarh in central India. My grandmother was a wonderful storyteller; when I was a child, she told us stories every night. After dinner, all the children of the extended family would fight with each other for a place next to Grandmother—we all wanted to sleep as close to her as possible, so that we didn't miss anything.

Grandmother was very expressive. When she told a story, her moods and expressions changed in keeping with the plot—sometimes she would laugh, if there was a funny bit, or she would start shedding tears if it was sad. When we listened to her, we felt that whatever she was telling us was happening right there in front of us, and we would begin to feel the same way about the characters and situations as she did. One of her favourite themes was the tiger. I think this is why the tiger is so real to me—even though I have never seen one truly in the wild, only in national parks or zoos. But my grandmother's stories about the beast and the forest are so vivid in my memory that I feel I know the creature.

Apart from Grandmother's fantastic stories, I also grew up with accounts of real life encounters with tigers, which were part of village lore. When I was very small, I heard the story of a family of tigers chancing on a herd of buffaloes. They did not attack immediately, appearing wary of going for an entire herd. But after a while, a lone tigress pounced on a buffalo, brought him down and threw him towards the others. *'That's because she had her cubs with her,'* explained the villager who told me this story. *'A tigress is aggressive when she has her cubs with her.'*

Some people had direct experience of the tiger's wrath. My aunt told me this story: her uncle had once taken his cows to graze into the deep forest, when a tiger attacked his herd and

injured him. He began to shout and scream—and thankfully, some people passing by heard him, and came to his rescue. They chased the tiger away and brought him back home. But the tiger was so angry that her prey had escaped that she followed the men, all the way to the village! She roared and circled around the house of the injured man—until the villagers all came out together to chase her out. *'Once a tiger scents a prey, she can't leave it alone, that's why she followed the injured man and his friends to the village.'* my aunt concluded.

I remember another story an uncle of mine told me. At one time, he was working for the forest department, and spent a lot of time moving around the jungle. One day he saw a tiger dragging a wild boar it had killed along the river bank. The tiger was thirsty and wanted to drink water, but he didn't want to lose sight of his meal... even for a moment! Even after he came down to the river to drink, he would look up after every sip, to check on the dead boar. He didn't want to leave it unguarded.

Such stories became part of my imagination, and I have continued to be fascinated by this powerful creature. I decided to write and illustrate this book of tiger tales, not just to add to the lore that already exists, but to bring in my own perspective as a Gond, whose ancestors actually lived with tigers roaming around not too far from where they lived.

To recall that time is to recall a world that has disappeared. Back then the Gond and the tiger had a common home—the forest—and the tiger was like an elder, a worthy ancestor. Gond memories of the tiger are unique: it was a creature to be feared, revered, and appeased. The tiger was considered so powerful that it even had magical powers. There are many Gond tales about tigers, and also Gond versions of well-known stories. What they all have in common is the close relationship that human beings had with tigers, and these are the stories I would like to remember, and pass on.

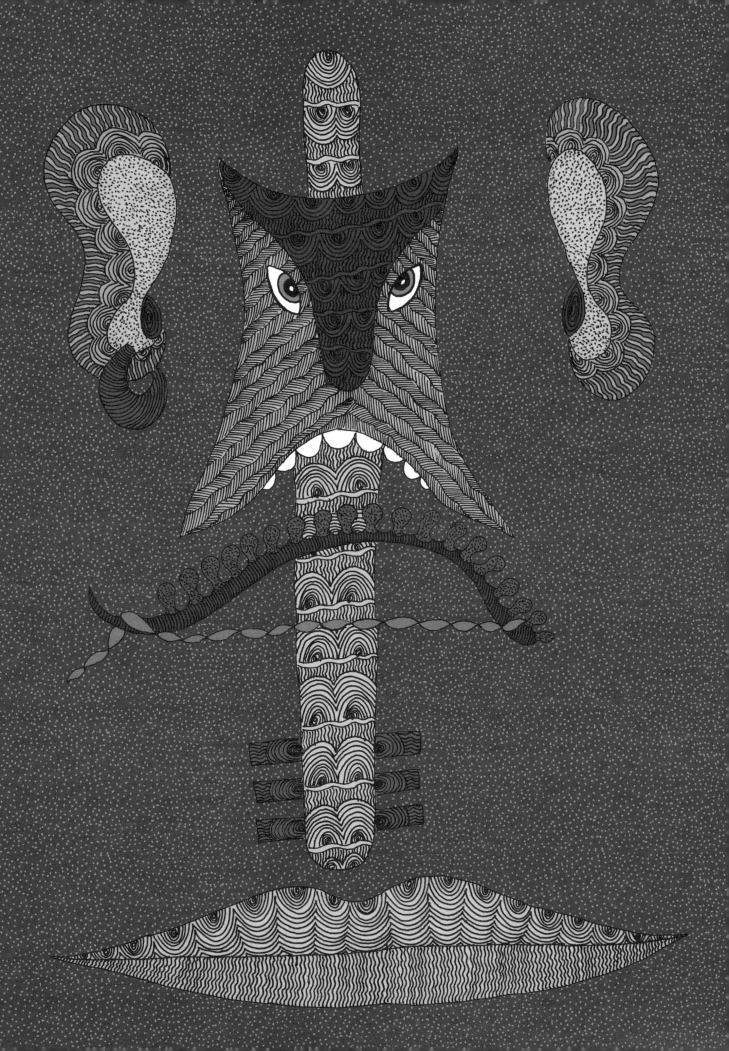

The Tiger God

IN THE OLDEN DAYS, amongst all the Gonds, it was the Khushram clan which feared and revered the tiger the most. So much so that the tiger was thought to be a great god called Bagaisur. Whenever there was a Khushram wedding in the village, Bagaisur turned up. But not as himself—he used his magic to enter into one of the family members. Possessed of the tiger's spirit, that person would not let the marriage rituals proceed. He would pounce on the sacred pot which is used in marriage ceremonies, and not rest until he destroyed it.

That was when an elder in the family came up with a plan: to save the sacred pot from Bagaisur, they should offer the possessed man something else. How about sacrificing a pig? Everyone agreed. Bagaisur was pleased with this arrangement and decided to leave the sacred pot alone. From that day onward, no Khushram wedding is complete without a pig being sacrificed to the Tiger God, Bagaisur.

What the Tiger Fears

THERE WAS A TIME when the tiger was friends with dogs and cats. At that time, they all lived in the wild. One day, a tiger tracked down a boar and killed it. But he didn't want to eat it raw. So he asked his friend, a dog, to go to the nearest village and fetch him a flame, so that he could roast the boar. The dog agreed and made his way to the nearest village.

As he neared the place, a faint aroma of something tasty tickled his nostrils. So he followed the smell and found himself in front of a hut. Outside the door, he discovered some scraps of food lying around—they seemed to be leftovers from a feast. The dog was excited. *'So much to eat! I should just live here. Why bother going back? Finding food is too much work in the forest—sniffing around all day to find something to hunt. This is easier!'* And so he made the village his home and forgot all about the tiger's request.

Meanwhile, the tiger waited for the dog to appear with a flame. One day passed, and another, and another, and another... but there was no sign of the dog. So the tiger turned to a cat, and asked him to go and fetch him a flame from the village. The cat was not too keen, but he agreed to go.

He reached the village, and wondered what to do next. Suddenly, he felt his nostrils quiver—something was smelling good! He followed the scent, softly and stealthily, and came to a small hut—the door was open, and there was no one inside. He crept in... and found a pot of warm milk on a ledge. Here was a meal! He leapt onto the ledge, and drank until he could drink no more. He was too full to move, so he dropped off the ledge, and curled himself into a corner of the hut. He decided that this is where he would remain—in the village. For there were other huts close to this one, and each hut, he was sure, would have a pot of milk.

Meanwhile, the tiger was tired of waiting. He was also worried about his friends, and began to have doubts about what he had done. Maybe he was wrong to send them out—what if the flame had singed them or roasted them alive? Such thoughts began to make him more and more anxious, until he got into such a state that the very idea of fire made him panic. Why, the flame could scorch him as well!

So from that day onward, he decided that he would rather eat his prey raw. And that is also why he always avoids a fire.

The Tiger's Gift

THE PARDHAN IS THE SINGER and storyteller in a Gond village. He is sent for by people who want him to perform the rituals needed to worship the great god, Badadev. All Gonds need to worship Badadev, even the most wealthy and powerful landowners amongst them, like the Thakurs.

One day a powerful Thakur from a distant village sent for a Pardhan to come and perform the prayer rituals in his house. The Pardhan set out, taking his instrument—the *bana*—with him. It was a long way to walk, and he had to pass through a dense forest. He walked the entire day, and as night fell, decided to sleep in the jungle. He gathered firewood and soon had a crackling fire going. Only then did he feel safe, for no animal dared come close to a fire.

The Pardhan was tired, but he felt that he had to pray to Badadev before he fell asleep. So he picked up his bana and started strumming. Enchanted by the music, a group of tigers came out of their caves, and sat around him, listening. After he had finished, each of them got up and offered him ornaments of gold and silver, which had been worn by people that the tigers had killed. The Pardhan was overwhelmed. He was moved by the tigers' offerings: *'No Thakur is going to give me such gifts!'* he said to himself. He decided to go back home, rather than visit the Thakur.

The Thakur was puzzled, and sent for the Pardhan again. And this time around too, the man's music had the tigers out and waiting with gifts. The Pardhan then decided that he would not visit or sing at the Thakur's house ever again. This custom is followed to this day.

Can a Cow and a Tiger be Friends?

A PARDHAN WAS ONCE gifted a cow. He brought the animal back to his house and tied her up in his courtyard. Since he had only this one cow, he did not take her out to graze. Instead, he brought her a bundle of grass every day. The cow was happy enough with this arrangement. She took to staying in the courtyard, munching and chewing her cud.

The sight of a content cow who had nothing to do angered the Pardhan's wife. She complained to her husband that the cow was lazy, that she couldn't bear the sight of the animal in the courtyard. She threatened to walk out of the house, if the cow was not sent away.

So the next morning, the Pardhan led the cow to the forest and left her there. The cow, who was pregnant, was unsure about what to do next. By and by, a tigress wandered into the place. She was also pregnant, and seeing the cow in a similar condition, decided not to attack her, but to be friends with her instead.

A few days later, both animals gave birth. Each would feed her little one, and then leave to find food for herself. The calf and the tiger cub grew up together and became good friends.

Soon it was summer. It was hot and not easy to find prey, so the tigress took to roaming around the river bank, her stomach rumbling with hunger. One day she saw her friend, the cow, drinking water a little further upstream. The tigress bent down to drink, but even though she filled her stomach with water, her hunger would not go away. Suddenly, she had the feeling that the water tasted different—was it because it was flowing from the cow's mouth? If the water from the cow's mouth tastes so good, the tigress thought to herself, how much better would her flesh taste?

So she went up to the cow and told her that she was just too hungry, and saw no other way out except to eat her. But since they had been friends, she would not kill her immediately, but would give her a day's time. The cow was stricken. She called out to her calf and told him what was to happen. From now on, she said, he had to learn to look after himself.

The next morning, the tiger killed and ate the cow. Satisfied with her large meal, she called her cub over and said that she was ready to feed him as well. But the cub was shocked and angry at what his mother had done.

22

He made a plan: a few days later, he asked his mother to teach him how to hunt and kill prey. The tigress was delighted and taught him all the skills she knew. The cub practised hard and one day, when he felt confident, he pounced on his mother... and killed her. He felt satisfied at his revenge, and went back to his friend the calf.

The two friends decided to live together.

One day, a hunter chanced upon the calf when he was alone... and killed him. He called out to his fellow hunters, and together, they prepared to carry him to the village. Just as they were ready to go, a young tiger stood in their path. It was the calf's friend. He told them that he wouldn't let them go until they gathered wood, built a fire, and roasted their meat right there. The hunters were afraid of the tiger, and did as they were told. As they lit the fire and began to roast the calf, they were shocked by what happened next. The young tiger jumped into the crackling flames, to join his friend, and the hunters watched in horror as both the creatures burned, and there was nothing left but ashes.

But a month after, two bamboo stalks grew out of the pile of ash that lay in the middle of the forest.

The Tiger's Reputation

THERE WAS ONCE a cowherd who liked to let his cow graze in the forest. He particularly liked to take her to a river that flowed through the jungle. While his cow grazed on the river bank, he would wander the length of the river, marvelling at its beauty.

One day, as he was strolling around, he was startled to see a tiger on the river bank. The animal seemed busy turning over a large stone. Even though the cowherd was scared of the tiger, he was curious about what was going on, and inched closer to get a better look. It looked as though the beast had got hold of a large crab from under the stone! The tiger crushed the crab, then laid it aside, and moved on to the next stone. Sure enough, there was a crab under that stone as well. But this time, things didn't go so well. Just as the tiger stretched out his paw to get it, the crab leapt onto his face... and bit the tiger on the nose! Not content with that, it crawled up, and slipped into his nostrils.

The tiger roared with pain. Helpless and angry, he let out a loud sneeze, to blow the crab out. But it didn't work. He shook his head, and clawed at his nose... nothing would get the crab out of his nose.

Watching the tiger writhing in pain, the cowherd took pity on him. Overcoming his fear of the huge beast, he walked up to him. Then he reached gently into his nose, took hold of the crab, pulled it out, and flung it away.

The tiger was overcome with relief and gratitude. He thanked the cowherd, but in a shame-faced way. *'Please don't tell anyone that the crab got into my nose. I'm supposed to be strong and powerful! Imagine how the other animals would laugh if they knew a crab had got the better of me!'*

The cowherd swore that he would not tell anyone. Now that he had done his good deed, he began to feel afraid of the tiger again. All he wanted to do was leave the river bank, take his cow and return home safely.

The tiger watched him leave. He was still concerned about his reputation—would the cowherd keep his word? Or would he gossip with his fellow villagers? That wouldn't do at all! The tiger decided to keep an eye on the cowherd. So he slipped into the village and hid himself in a bush behind the cowherd's house. That way, he would be able to listen in on all the conversations going on in the house.

But in fact the cowherd had every intention of keeping his promise to the tiger. He wasn't thinking of telling anyone the story of the crab at all. But did the tiger trust his word? He didn't think so. The cowherd had a strange feeling that he was being watched... every time he left his hut, he felt scared for some reason. The tiger must be hiding close by, watching him. Sometimes he had a feeling that he was right behind him, shadowing his every step. But he dared not turn and look!

One morning, the cowherd heard a rustling sound in the bush behind his hut. The tiger! The cowherd felt he had had enough... it was time to take action. He set a pot of water on the fire to boil, and when the water was really hot, he took it off the fire carefully. He then stepped softly over to the back of his hut, and taking careful aim, flung the boiling water into the bush. He heard a yelp, and ran back into his house. From that day onwards, he stopped being afraid. Perhaps the tiger has learnt his lesson, he told himself.

Tiger-man

THERE WAS ONCE a poor woodcutter who had three daughters. He made a living by going into the forest everyday, to cut down dead wood from tree branches. He would carry the sticks back to the village, and sell them as firewood. One day, after cutting wood, he found that he was too tired to haul it all back to the village. He shouted for help, but no one heard him, since he was deep inside the forest. He waited and called out again, but there was still no response. Finally, angry and tired, he cried, *'Whoever helps to carry these logs of wood home, I'll marry my eldest daughter to him!'*

A tiger hidden in the deep bushes heard him. Using his magical powers to change into a man, he appeared in front of the woodcutter and offered to carry his logs for him. The woodcutter was pleased and the two made their way to the village. Then, as promised, the woodcutter married his daughter to the stranger who had helped him.

The two walked back to the forest, hand in hand. As they passed a tall tree, a bird sang out: *'Don't go into the land of the tiger, for the tiger will eat you!'* The girl was puzzled. *'What's the bird saying? I'm not sure I understood!'*

'Oh, that's nothing. Birds and animals in the forest speak in different voices and we don't know what they're saying. Pay the bird no heed. We have a long way to go, let's walk on."

And so the two walked further into the forest.

At one point, the man stopped. *'I'm thirsty. I'll go and fetch some water. You stay here!'* The girl was scared, but agreed.

A few minutes later, the girl was startled on seeing a tiger. But before she could do anything, the tiger pounced on her and killed her.

Some days later, the tiger changed shape once again to become a man and visited the woodcutter's house. *'Your daughter has taken ill. Could you please send her sister to nurse her?'* The woodcutter agreed, and his second daughter went along with her sister's husband.

As they walked into the forest, the girl was startled to hear a birdcall. The bird seemed to be sounding a warning. She turned to the man and asked him what that meant. Just as he had done earlier, he asked her to ignore the bird and walk on. And as before, he went in search of water, and returned, changed into a tiger. The girl was terrified, but before she could say or do anything, she was eaten.

Once again, the tiger-turned-man visited the woodcutter and demanded that he send his youngest—and only remaining—daughter with him. The woodcutter agreed. On the way, this sister too was greeted with a warning song. But she was asked to ignore it. Deep in the forest, the man left her to drink water.

Unlike her sisters, the youngest was a curious girl. She looked around and saw that there were sparkling ornaments strewn all round her.

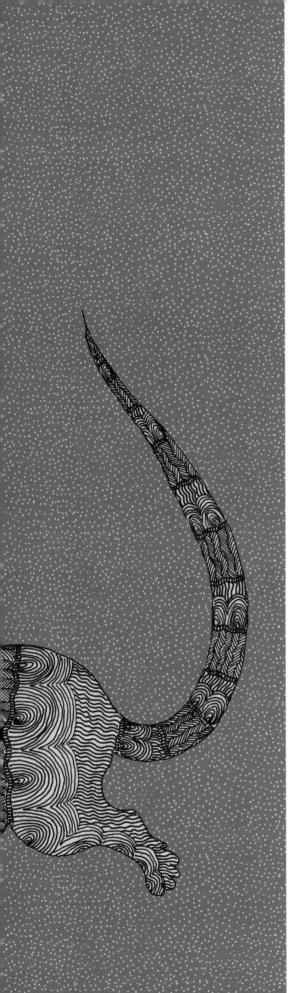

She recognised some of them—they were her sisters' jewellery! She remembered the bird's warning song and realised that something was very wrong.

Before the tiger could appear, she ran as fast as she could back to the village and told her father the whole story. The woodcutter realised that the man who visited his house, asking for his daughters, was no ordinary man. *'He'll come again, I'm sure! Well, this time I'll be ready for him!'* said the woodcutter.

The tiger-turned-man turned up a few hours later. He said he had lost his sister-in-law in the forest and wondered if she had returned home. *'She's here, as you can see!'* said the woodcutter. The girl turned to the visitor and asked him if he would like to freshen up. *'You look tired! You'll surely like a warm bath!'* The tiger-man was happy enough to be fussed over, and agreed.

He waited in the backyard for the water. And then, when he was least expecting it, a pot of boiling hot water was hurled at him. And as the water drenched him, his skin changed colour, and he changed form. In the place of the man stood a tiger.

Enraged, the woodcutter threw yet another pot of hot water on the animal. Scalded and burnt, the tiger tried to fight back, but was no match for the two human beings.

The woodcutter and his daughter heaved a sigh of relief.

Imagining the Tiger

MY FOUR YEAR OLD SON, Chalit, loves to play with me. One of our favourite games is the tiger game in which he is the tiger and I am his prey. *'I'll bite you!'* he roars, and starts to chase me around the house. I try to run away from him, and this makes him laugh. When Chalit turns into a tiger, he opens his mouth wide, bares his teeth, and comes at me with his hands splayed like claws... he is ready for his victim, and does everything he can to frighten me.

Chalit's teacher has taught him that T is for tiger, and told him that the beast lives in the forest, that he is the king of all animals, and that he roars. Chalit has been to the local zoo with me (for we live in the city now and the forest is far away). We have gone looking for the tiger at the zoo many times—and found him hidden behind a tree or rock. Sometimes only his tail is visible, at other times, one of his paws. He stays within the boundaries of the area around which he is allowed to wander. Visitors come in large numbers to see him, and like Chalit, are happy if they actually manage to spot him.

Each time we leave the zoo, I wonder if Chalit will be able to retain that sense of excitement he experiences when he spots the tiger. For we live in a world where everyone is running to get ahead, and leave others behind. Such a life does not leave you with much time for remembering. This is why I have put down these stories from many decades ago when talk about tigers was common in Patangarh, our village. They are from a time when the tiger was free to roam, and human beings needed to negotiate living in close quarters with such a powerful creature. These tiger tales are part of our common memory—of reverence, awe and fear—and I would like these stories to be remembered.

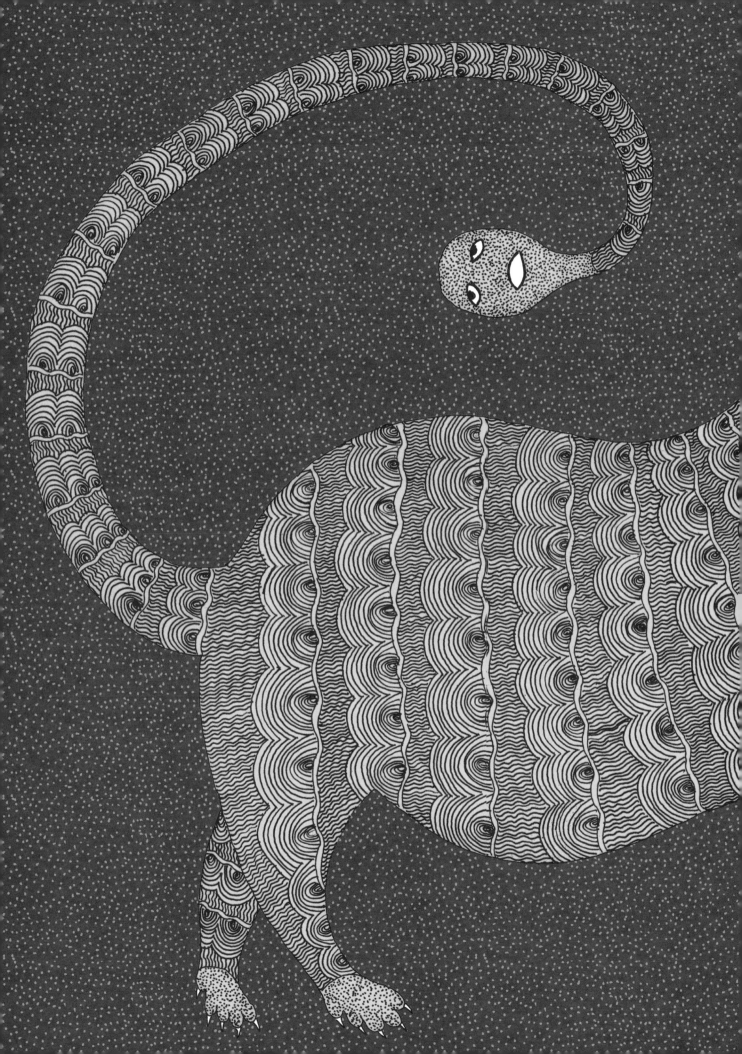